DESERT BIFF

CHRIS GARRATT & MICK KIDD

CORGI BOOKS

Many thanks to Chris Render of Pavement Press for all his help and support

DESERT ISLAND BIFF

A CORGI BOOK 0 552 12685 3

First publication in Great Britain

PRINTING HISTORY

Corgi edition published 1985

Corgi Books are published by Transworld Publishers Ltd., Century House, 61–63 Uxbridge Road, Ealing, London W5 5SA, in Australia by Transworld Publishers (Aust.) Pty. Ltd., 26 Harley Crescent, Condell Park, NSW 2200, and in New Zealand by Transworld Publishers (N.Z.) Ltd., Cnr. Moselle and Waipareira Avenues, Henderson, Auckland.

Made and printed in Great Britain by Thomson Litho Ltd., East Kilbride, Scotland

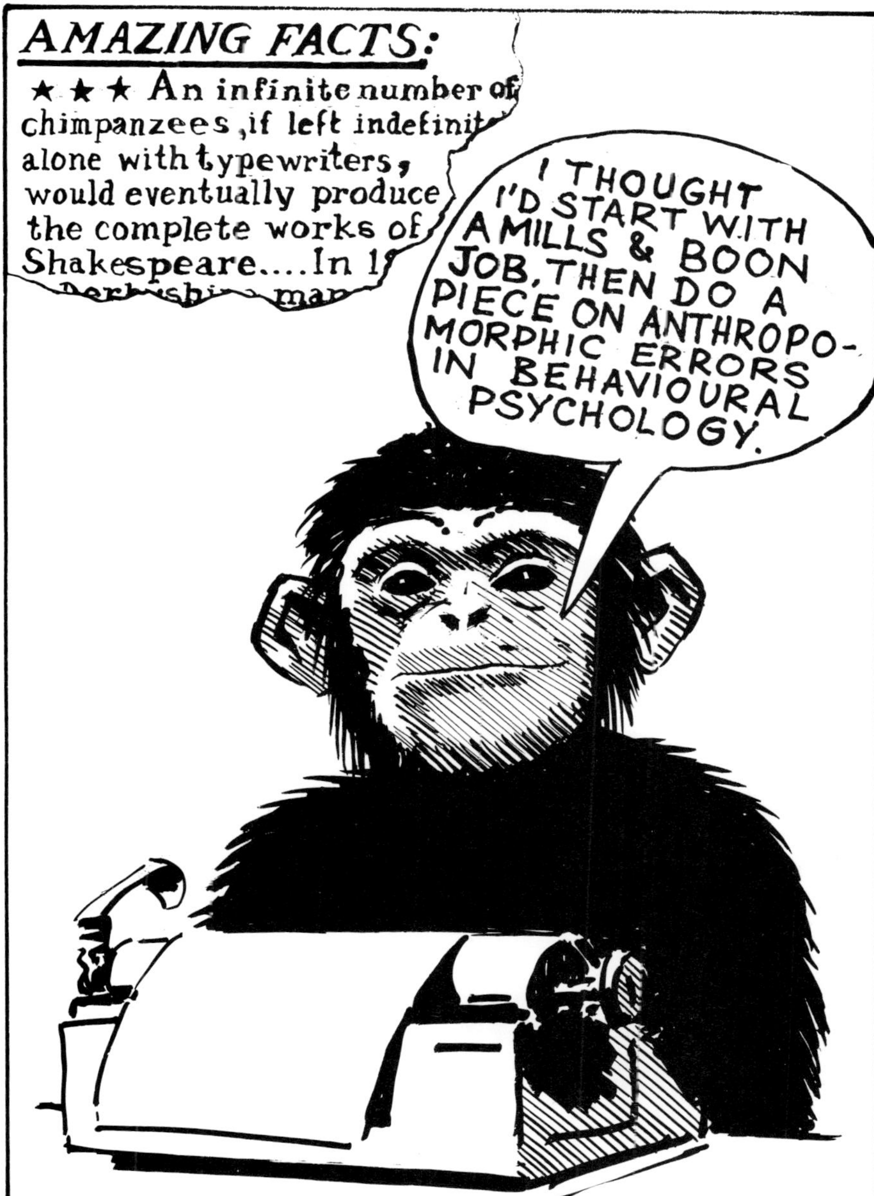
AMAZING FACTS:
★★★ An infinite number of chimpanzees, if left indefinit alone with typewriters, would eventually produce the complete works of Shakespeare....In 1
I THOUGHT I'D START WITH A MILLS & BOON JOB, THEN DO A PIECE ON ANTHROPO-MORPHIC ERRORS IN BEHAVIOURAL PSYCHOLOGY.

LIVES OF THE ARTISTS No 1:
'ONLY THE LONELY'
THE BIG O's SMASH HIT
INSPIRES THIS PATHETIC STORY OF INNER AGONY — GUARANTEED TO BRING AN ACHE TO YOUR HEART OR YOUR MONEY BACK!
HI THERE! MEET THE GUY THEY USED TO CALL THE PENMAN OF ENNUI... HARRY BRENT'S THE NAME, CARTOONING IS MY GAME!
STATUTORY BERET
Adrian Hill
"IT ALL STARTED WITH A TINY AD. IN THE PAPER..."
FOR SALE Machine removing chewing gum from carpets. Bargain
STUDIO SPACE
VISUAL ARTS
"Anyone Can Draw With This Amazing Invention—Instantly!"
- says famous artist David Hockney
landscapes portraits still lives minimalism conceptual post-modernism romanticism etc.
actual size
40p +15p postage
Muggins Supplies
Ideal for
best selling novels, breeding, tool storage etc. A boon to D.I.Y. enthusiasts. £180 o.n.o 76415 (after 6p
"SOON, I WAS FOREGOING MANY SOCIAL OCCASIONS."
ALL SET TO GO CLUBBING, HARRY?
EXPRESSO BONGO
IL RONDO
JIVE DIVE
COFFEE
NOT TONIGHT; —I'M STAYING IN TO GRAPPLE WITH MY IMPASTO TECHNIQUE. HAVE A TIA MARIA FOR ME.

"...SUDDENLY, I WAS HOOKED!"
YOU'RE NOT STILL DOODLING IN THE LEDGERS, ARE YOU, HARRY? WHERE ARE THOSE FIGURES I BUZZED YOU FOR THIS MORNING?
"Birth of Science"
Inner Echoes
ZOOM!
WHIRR
WHIRR
"...I WANT TO BE A DREAMER AWAKE..." -SORRY BOSS, WHAT WAS THAT? -OH SURE, I'LL GET THEM AT ONCE!
"OF COURSE THERE WERE TIMES WHEN IT ALL CAME TOGETHER IN A CREATIVE RUSH"..
I'VE CRACKED IT! ....YOU SEE BOSS, THE AIM IS TO ACHIEVE A NEGATION OF BALANCE BETWEEN SPACE AND FORM, SO THAT THE IMAGE IS IMBUED WITH A SENSE OF DRAMATIC TORMENT.
THE MOUNTAIN OF LIFE H.BRENT '85
REALLY? HOW FASCINATING. -YOU'RE FIRED, HARRY.
DISQUE BLEU
Brent
Brent
"...TIMES WHEN I FELT I'D MADE THE WRONG CAREER MOVE—"
I LIKE YOU, HARRY— I LIKE YOU A LOT.... BUT THERE'S NO FUTURE FOR US..IT'S HOPELESS.
CUT! OKAY EVERYONE, WE'LL BREAK THERE FOR LUNCH.
LOOK—CALL OFF THE GORILLAS... I'LL APPROACH UNITED TECHNOLOGIES FOR SPONSORSHIP FIRST THING MONDAY MORNING.
KEN RUSSELL
"THAT'S WHEN I JUST CRAVED NORMALITY..."
THAT'S ALL, THAT'S ALL.
?
FANTASTIC ISN'T IT? —AND THE WARMTH OF THE PEOPLE WILL REMAIN WITH US LONG AFTER OUR TANS HAVE FADED!

"...TO BE FREE FROM RIDICULE AND THE MERCILESS TAUNTING OF SOCIETY."
...NO, SERIOUSLY, – I REALLY LIKE HARRY'S WORK... IN FACT I'VE GOT ONE OF HIS DRAWINGS HANGING IN THE BOG.
RICHARD CLAYDERMA IN CONCERT
HO-HO! – DON'T TELL US WHAT YOU USE IT FOR!
FUME
BAR
HEY! – IS THIS WHAT THEY CALL LAVATORY HUMOUR?
"LATER I WAS AFFLICTED BY A CRISIS OF STYLE."
WHAT IS IT, HARRY? YOU CAN TELL ME.
I CAN'T DECIDE WHETHER TO GO FOR TORTURED ANGULARITY OR FREE-FLOWING BLOBS ANY MORE.
UNFITTED CARPET
"WHEN IT GOT BAD, I WOULD GO OUT, GRAB A BITE, AND TALK ABOUT ANYTHING EXCEPT THE ANXIETY OF MAKING A MARK!"
...SO I TOLD THIS GUY – JOKING OF COURSE – ...AH... ARE WE READY TO ORDER?... I HOPE YOU DON'T MIND GOING DUTCH, BY THE WAY – I'VE A BIT OF A CASH FLOW PROBLEM RIGHT NOW.
IN THAT CASE, SIR, MAY I RECOMMEND THE SPAGHETTI HOOPS?
TAKE AWAY SERVICE AVAILABLE
Menu
HOTEL DE POSH
IAN BREAKWELL'S DIARIES
"BUT I LEARNED TO TAKE THE ROUGH WITH THE SMOOTH AND, ABOVE ALL, REMAIN OPEN TO CHANGE AND CONSTRUCTIVE CRITICISM"
...YOU SEE, HARRY, YOU'RE STILL TALKING ABOUT THE HEGEMONY OF ART AS IF IT'S ABOVE THE SOCIAL ORDER –
– WHICH IS AN ESSENTIALLY REACTIONARY STANCE!

"THAT NIGHT, IN MY STUDIO..."
YES - THEY'RE RIGHT.. MY WORK IS AN OX-BOW LAKE IN THE RIVER OF RELEVANCE! TIME FOR A RADICAL RETHINK......(THINKS)..
CUBISM REDEFINED
PAINT AS PAINT
Minimal art. Vol 9
TO LET
THIS IS IT! THE NEW COMMITTED ME! THE ANGRY LINE - THE SAVAGE EYE.... RELENTLESS SATIRE ERODING THE CANKERED FACADE OF THE BOURGEOISIE WITH VITRIOLIC VERSE AND CAUSTIC CARICATURE!
"I'M NOT SAYING I'M ENTIRELY FREE OF INDIVIDUALISM - I STILL HAVE DELUSIONS OF GRANDEUR I GUESS..."
HEY EVERYBODY, WE HAVE US A BIRTHDAY BOY HERE TONIGHT, WHOSE BUSY PEN STROKES, COAXING LIFE FROM MISTINESS AND MURK, CONTAIN ESSENCES OF LATE TURNER!
IS THIS YOUR DOING?
C'MON UP, BIG FELLAH!
BUT I STILL STRIVE FOR INNOCENCE AND INTEGRITY.. - IS THAT THING SWITCHED ON BY THE WAY?
CRACKLE - THE BAR AND BUFFET WILL BE CLOSING IN FIVE MINUTES.
125 mph
JOURNALIST
WOULD YOU SAY YOUR NEW WORK WAS IN DANGER OF TRADING IN FALSE PARTICULARS AND PRESUMED ASSENT?
THE END.

ON THE SCENE

THE INVITATION
I DON'T GO TO PARTIES ON PRINCIPLE — ON THE PRINCIPLE THAT MY ABSENCE WILL BE MORE NOTEWORTHY THAN MY PRESENCE....
MOM
I COULD STAY IN AND GROW A BEARD.
Expressive Mime
Illusionary Mime
NEXT ON THE BOX WE HAVE HARD-TRAVELLIN' DAVE ATTENBOROUGH, CROSSING CONTINENTS IN MID-SENTENCE WITHOUT CHANGING HIS SAFARI SUIT.
DIET-FREE PINACOLADA
"...PROBABLY BE FULL OF PEOPLE NAME-DROPPING..."
IN ACTUAL FACT, I STAYED IN THE SAME HOTEL ROOM THAT JIM MORRISON DIED IN!
-LARRY PARNES, HARRY WEBB, DUFFY POWER, WEEDON, — I'VE WORKED WITH ALL OF 'EM!
'COURSE, YOU WOULDN'T REMEMBER THE PERFUMED GARDEN WOULD YOU?
"...OR MAYBE IT'LL BE SOME HIGHBROW AFFAIR...."
IS THERE A TELLY SOMEWHERE? I HAVE TO WATCH THE SKY AT NIGHT.
...THINK I'LL MOSEY OVER TO THE HOLOGRAM ROOM..
WEATHER REPORT
SANDY YOU MUST MEET GAVIN, HE'S A HISTORIAN.
WONDERFUL! TELL ME - WHAT DO YOU KNOW ABOUT TALLYRAND'S FOREIGN POLICY?
"...WORSE - I MIGHT BE EXPECTED TO BE A RAVER..."
I DON'T DANCE!
ANYONE FOR MAH JONG?
WHY DON'T WE ALL EXPRESS OURSELVES VIA BODY LANGUAGE?
CLICK!
"... OR GET EMBROILED WITH A LATE-NIGHT RACONTEUR IN THE KITCHEN."
HI! HAVE SOME YEASTVITE! DID YOU KNOW, BY THE WAY, THAT THE PARISIAN SEWER SYSTEM IS TEEMING WITH PERSON-EATING ALLIGATORS WHICH HAVE GROWN UP FROM BABY ONE FLUSHED DOWN THE BOG AS UNWANTED PETS?
"...BUT THEN - I MIGHT MEET... THE ONE"
Libra- Money matters take a back seat at the weekend; meanwhile, on the romantic front, you're laughing.
IN RENDERING WOMEN THE AESTHETIC SEX, MEN ALSO RENDER THEM THE SUBORDINATE SEX, MEAT-HEAD.
NEWSPAPER HOROSCOPES ARE BUNK ANYWAY.

REMEMBER THE CLUB-A-GO-GO?
YEAH, - I WAS ON THE HOLLIES GUEST LIST AT ONE TIME.
THE CABARET BEGINS IN FIVE MINUTES AND FEATURES AN AGIT-PROP MIME TROUPE AND SOME ACAPELLA GLOVE PUPPETS...
WHATEVER'S WRONG, HONEY?
NOTHING... IT'S JUST THAT I'VE BEEN INVITED TO SEE A BAND WHICH IS DESCRIBED AS "INDISPENSABLE TO ANYONE WITH A POST-PUNK SENSIBILITY," AND I'VE NEVER EVEN HEARD OF THEM!

IT'S Tea and chat TIME AGAIN FOR THE UNEXPECTED GUEST
TINA! AMAZING! ...LET ME DRINK YOU IN!
OH, HI BRIAN. I WAS JUST LEAVING THE COUNTRY.
I WON'T KEEP YOU MORE THAN 4 HOURS... I JUST WANT TO SNEAK BEHIND YOUR DEFENCE MECHANISMS A LITTLE.
THANKS... SORRY ABOUT THIS...TOO MANY LATE NIGHTS...
3 HOURS LATER..
WORDS ARE SO USELESS... WE MUST BREAK THROUGH THE BARRIERS OF LANGUAGE THAT DRAW US CLOSE BUT KEEP US APART....
THIS IS DEFINITELY OUT OF ORDER.
8 HOURS LATER
I'M TIRED OF ALL THESE GENDER GAMES. WHY CAN'T WE JUST BE... WHOEVER.... WHEREVER... WHENEVER...
I'VE GOT TO SAY SOMETHING... SO MUCH FOR MY ASSERTIVENESS TRAINING!
ZZZZZ
3 DAYS LATER...
..IT'S NOT THE WORDS SO MUCH AS THE SILENT SPACES BETWEEN THEM THAT I WANT TO EXPLORE. I MEAN – WHAT DID YOU THINK WHEN I FIRST APPEARED? I'M FASCINATED ABOUT HOW WE COME ACROSS!
STOP WALLYING ME OUT!
OH BRIAN!
NEXT YEAR...
....WELL, I'VE KEPT YOU LONG ENOUGH; I GUESS YOU MUST HAVE THINGS TO DO.
THANKS FOR A FABULOUS MONOLOGUE, BRIAN. DO YOU MIND KICKING THE MILK BOTTLES OVER ON YOUR WAY OUT?
ANY RESEMBLANCE TO REAL PEOPLE IS DUE TO THE EXISTENCE OF AN ACAUSAL PRINCIPLE.

FLATSHARE
5TH PERSON SOUGHT BY RELAXED COLLECTIVE IN DOG-FREE ZONE. OWN SPACE, AVOCADO TILED BATHROOM. NON-SMOKER PREFERRED. REPLIES - BOX 671.
WELL, DO YOU HAVE ANY QUESTIONS YOU'D LIKE TO ASK US?
WELL, YES - JUST ONE OR TWO: 1. WHAT, IF ANY, UNRESOLVED TENSIONS EXIST BETWEEN YOU AS A DYNAMIC? 2. DO YOU BAN TAKEAWAY CARTONS FROM THE COOKING AREA? 3. IS THIS THE KIND OF PLACE I COULD BRING MY PARENTS BACK TO? 4. IS THERE ANYONE WHO LEAVES THE LIGHTS ON ALL NIGHT OR PISSES ON THE LAVATORY SEAT?

PHIL AND DON'S
'LIKE STRANGERS' INSPIRES THIS POIGNANT YARN
THE NIGHT IS YOUNG – LET'S GO TO THE PICTURES!
I CAN'T TONIGHT, SAM, – I'M DOING MY HAIR.
THANKS SUE... AND OVER TO YOU KIERON
Murder in the Collective
SETTIN GEL
Bonemeal & Catshit SHAMPOO
SAY I'M NOT HERE.
...HANG ON – LET ME CHECK MY DIARY.... NO MONDAY'S OUT, – THAT'S MY DISCUSSION CIRCLE.
..PITY – I KNOW THIS KNOCKOUT WINE BAR THAT'S ABSOLUTELY JAM-PACKED SINCE IT GOT HIGHLY RECOMMENDED.
HOW ABOUT TUESDAY?
– BABYSITTING... THURSDAY?
THAT'S THE VIDEO WORKSHOP.. I COULD DO A WEEK ON WEDNESDAY..
AH – NATURAL DANCE CLASS... HOW ABOUT TUESDAY 19TH?
THAT'S MY EMBASSY NIGHT... ..SATURDAY 23RD?
SORRY – I STAY IN SATURDAYS TO CONFRONT THE SOCIAL PRESSURES TO GO OUT... SUNDAY?
NO – THAT'S WHEN MY PARENTS ARE COMING... HOW DOES MARCH LOOK, SO FAR?
WELL, I CAN PENCIL YOU IN FOR THE 11TH.. NO – HANG ON...
– ONE DAY IN MAY...
WELL, IT WAS GREAT SEEING YOU... BUT I SHOULD BE GETTING BACK – I'VE GOT A MEETING OF THE STEERING COMMITTEE.
ME TOO... I THINK I LEFT THE BATH RUNNING.
DALE MART
Man's Wrap-Around
In 100% cotton terry towelling, blue with red trim and embroidered initials. 19" long, it has an elastic top and velcro fastening. It beats a towel bunched around the waist and is a real space saver when you travel.

EXISTENTIALIST JOKE No. 347.
LEADER OF THE PACK
THE TROUBLE WITH YOU, KEVIN, IS THAT YOU OVERLOOK THE ALL-DETERMINING CENTRALITY OF BEING-IN-THE-WORLD BECAUSE TO YOU, THE EVERYDAY ACTUALITIES OF THIS INHABITING ARE SO VARIOUS AND SEEMINGLY BANAL!
NOM D'UN NOM!
CAREFUL TERRY!
COME OUTSIDE AND SAY THAT!

STREET
LIFE
BAZ: PART ONE OF AN OCCASIONAL SERIES IN WHICH PEOPLE TALK ABOUT THEIR STYLE...
TYPICAL DAY:
GET UP....SLING BACK SOME COFFEE AND SOME BRAN....THEN POUND THE TYPE-KEYS UNTIL THE FIRST CRISIS OCCURS....
GRR! ALL MY PEERS ARE DOING VIDEO PROMOS OR LAYING DOWN TRACKS ON VINYL AND I'M STILL STUCK ON MY EXPLOSIVE CONTRO-VERSIAL FIRST CHAPTER!
CLATTER-CLATTER
WELL - HOW DID YOU BOYS GET STARTED?
WELL ANDY— WE JUST WALKED ON AND BEGAN OUR BRAND OF ANTI-MUSIC.... SINISTER DRUMBEAT, PRIMAL SCREAMS, DIDACTIC DISCOURSE, THAT KINDA STUFF..
HOME:
A LITTLE FLAT, SOUTH OF THE RIVER. TO RELAX, I LIKE TO MIX WITH SUCCESSFUL PEOPLE; BUT SOMETIMES I WONDER IF THEY REALLY KNOW ME AT ALL...
SAY BAZ - WHERE'S YOUR COMPUTERISED PHONE KEPT? I'VE GOT SOME COMMODITIES TO SHIFT ON THE SPOT MARKET.
NICE BIT OF REAL ESTATE YOU GOT HERE, BAZ....IS YOUR SWIMMING POOL IN THE ATTIC OR DOES YOUR ROOF NEED FIXING?
TV am
HI THERE...MY NAME IS PEGGY DEAN AND THIS IS MY ROOM-MATE PATRICK.
-Oh yes, I forgot... ...my bed was built out of wood from a crashed pier. It weighs 800 lbs.

TASTE/CLOTHES
I PREFER TO WORK WITH THE RADIO ON WHILST WEARING A DESIGNER BLAZER TO PRETEND I'M AT MY OFFICE. -OH YES, AND I'M FOND OF THE ODD SAMOSA...
...AND NOW- "CHANSON D'AUTOMNE" IN WHICH THE POET COMPARES HIMSELF TO A FALLING LEAF ABOUT TO LAND IN SOME DOGSHIT...
Chapter One
—DON'T PANIC.... GIVE IT TIME... HAVE ANOTHER COFFEE... -REMEMBER, IT TOOK FLAUBERT THREE WEEKS TO WRITE ONE LINE!
ALL TRANSISTOR RADIO
ROMANCE/TRAVEL
I MAINLY RIDE THE FREIGHT TRAIN OF MY MIND BUT LIZ AND I GRAB ONE HOLIDAY A YEAR. APART FROM THAT, I LIKE GO-GO DANCING TO KEEP FIT AND WOULD LIKE TO OWN A RACEHORSE.
F.8. SHOULD DO IT...
HURRY UP AND GET THE ICECREAMS, BAZ.
HOLD IT JUST LIKE THAT!
DO YOU WISH TO BECOME A STAR IN YOUR OWN LIVING ROOM?
Don't miss this opportunity of a lifetime..
no commitment,
no obligation whatsoever!
Everything by mail!
No salesman will call!
☐ YES! I want to consider this as a part- time self- -publicising opportunity.

HEARTLAND
"...ANTI-SEXIST PROFESSIONAL MAN WOULD LIKE TO MEET WOMAN FOR COUNTRY WALKS AND CUDDLES..."
WHAT RECENT BRITISH DRAMA HAVE YOU ENJOYED?
TSK! CITY SLICKERS!
HMM... NEEDS TO BE MORE SPECIFIC.
-HOW ABOUT, "EASY-GOING, UNCOMPLICATED GUY..." NO, -MIGHT APPEAR SELF--PROMOTING.
I'M THE ONLY PERSON I KNOW WHO'S NOT IN THERAPY THESE DAYS!
YOU WOULDN'T RECOGNISE A NEUROSIS EVEN IF ONE SHAT ON YOUR SHOULDER, YOU SMUG OAF.
"...MULTI-DIMENSIONAL SOCIALIST MAN, 30-ISH, INTERESTS INCLUDE SEMIOLOGY, CYCLING, HUMAN POTENTIAL, SELLING NEWSPAPERS, SOVIET CINEMA AND PINTING IT, WISHES TO LINK UP WITH FEMINIST TO EXPLORE IDEAS, FORM EQUAL FRIENDSHIP, MAYBE MORE....."
-OVERLONG... -MAKES ME SOUND LIKE A POLYMATH.
"...FASHION-CONSCIOUS BLOKE, KEEN TO SHARE LAUGHS WITH SIMILAR FEMALE..."
-SO THIS BARBER SAYS, "DON'T WORRY GUV, IT'S THE NEW LOOK!"
I DON'T GET IT.
I - YOUNG-AT-HEART, CARING MALE; YOU - FUNLOVING, INDEPENDENT FEMALE. TOGETHER WE-
-ACTUALLY I'M THE TOKEN WAITRESS.
Take-Away Menu Available
Reserved for Class of '68
AH.. BUGGER IT. WHY DON'T I JUST REPLY TO OTHER PEOPLE.
THAT'S THE TROUBLE WITH YOU YOUNG PEOPLE TODAY!
NEXT, DARTS ON 4, WITH MELVYN BRAGG.
Heartland

Here Comes Summer
DO YOU FANCY A DRIVE UNDER THE PALE MOONLIGHT?
AS LONG AS WE DON'T KISS, – IT MAKES MY FLAT-TOP CURL!
GETAWAY PEOPLE
SCHOOL'S NOT S'BAD BUT SUMMER'S BETTER..
WELL, ACTUALLY I'M 32, BUT I STILL READ THE FACE AND TAKE A 28" WAIST IN SLACKS.
THEY SAY THE RETSINA GROWS ON YOU AFTER YOUR TENTH BOTTLE.
18-30 CLUB

MODERN YOUTH IN SEARCH OF A TAKEAWAY
THESE LIVE-IN PARTNERS ARE ENJOYING A SOUL SHAKEDOWN PARTY WHEN...
I'M STARVING AFTER ALL THIS DANCING!
I'LL BELT OUT FOR SOME FOOD BEFORE WE START THE HULLY-GULLY.
HEY MAMBO MAMBO ITALIANO...
OUT IN THE MEAN STREETS, BARRY, A FORMER SHORT-ORDER COOK HIMSELF, CHECKS OUT A VARIETY OF FAST FOOD VENUES...
COME PRIMA...
WELL, IT WAS LOVELY, ALEX... BUT I'D HAVE BEEN JUST AS HAPPY WITH A SLAP-UP STAND-UP BUFFET...
...CANARIES POSSIBLY ALTHOUGH GOD KNOWS WHERE THE MONEY'S COMING
WEDDING PARTIES CATERED FOR
JUST MARRIED
SHALL WE KNOCK DOWN THE STRUCTURAL WALL OR PAINT THE BATHROOM FIRST?
...NOT THERE... -IT'S FULL OF NEWLYWEDS.
YEAH - IT'LL BE A RELENTLESSLY DEPRESSING FILM IN THE FLY-ON-THE-WALL, HAND-HELD CAMERA TRADITION ABOUT THE AWFULNESS OF HUMAN RELATIONSHIPS - ER, TWO DONER KEBABS PLEASE.
COME ON GRAEME, LET'S GO FOR IT!
WHY WERE WE ON THAT BUS? WE ONLY EVER TAKE TAXIS.
I'M THINKING OF TAKING A LOAD OF FLUORESCENT LOONS TO FLOG OFF AT GLASTONBURY.
OH YEAH, - GIVING THE SCENTED CANDLES A MISS THIS YEAR, THEN?
THIS ONE'S NO GOOD EITHER... ...OVER-TRENDY.
Special Presentation ONE NIGHT ONLY!! "YOU ARE WHAT YOU EAT +V.A.T." Street Level Theatre Co Subsidised by Moss Bros.
GOLDEN PRAWN CHINESE RESTAURANT
I CAUGHT YOUR LAUNDERETTE GIG - REALLY PACEY!
WE ARE NOT ACTORS AND YOU ARE NOT THE AUDIENCE: WE ARE ALL EXPLORING... ETC.
DAMN - IT'S SHUT!
?
NO CHIPS TONIGHT, SUNSHINE - THE FRYER CAUGHT FIRE THIS LUNCHTIME.
Cornish PASTIES 35P
PANCAKE ROLLS 40P
Stabbo Hygenic Hardwood Fish Forks
-HOPE I CAN KEEP THOSE SNAKEBITES DOWN.
I HAVE A MEAL EVERY NIGHT WITH THE REST OF THE FAMILY, AND THEN FOR MY SUPPER I NIP DOWN HERE FOR A LARGE CURRY.
I'M THE SAME WITH McVITIE'S HOMEWHEAT... I'M ON A PACKET A DAY!
CHICKEN MADRAS?
AT LAST! GOOD CHEAP FOOD WITH A NO-NONSENSE ATMOSPHERE!
IS IT POSSIBLE TO MADISON WHILST EATING A BIRIANI? STAY TUNED.

CONTINUING OUR SERIES FEATURING GREAT DUVETS OF THE WORLD:
landscapes of the mind
a slow-moving saga set behind ONE WOMAN'S FOREHEAD
-WELL, THAT'S ABOUT IT FOR TONIGHT ON BBC1. JUST STARTING ON BBC2 IS THE OPEN UNIVERSITY MODULE 4 ON DIFFERENTIAL CALCULUS. MEANWHILE, FOR ALL YOU NIGHT-OWLS, RADIO 2 CONTINUES THROUGHOUT THE NIGHT...
WELL, TIME FOR SOME SHUTEYE I GUESS.
LATER THAT SAME NIGHT...
...MUST TAKE MY BIORHYTHMS IN FOR AN M.O.T.
I KNEW I SHOULDN'T HAVE NIPPED OUT FOR THAT SPECIAL FRIED RICE WITH SWEET'N'SOUR SAUCE AND 5 SPRING ROLLS AT 11 O'CLOCK.
HI THERE, SLEEP-CHEATS, TIME FOR SOME MELLOW-TIME MUSIC HAWAIIAN STYLE AS THE CASCADING STRINGS SWING US GENTLY INTO TUESDAY WITH MALCOLM MARSHMALLOW'S ARRANGEMENT OF "ALOHA"...
TOSSING—
I COULD BE WORKING ON MY REPORT OR MAKING A PARTY TAPE.
DONG
...THE NEXT PROGRAMME ON BBC'S WORLD SERVICE IS FOR HUNGARIAN LISTENERS...
'N' TURNING
ZEEOWWZZ. ZZ RADIOZZZ ALBANIAAAOOW WWEEEEESHSH SHSH COMING UP TO HALF PAST FIVE BRBRRRRR SSSS FARMING REPORT CKCKCKC K CHIME SSSSS...
EVEN IF I DID FALL ASLEEP NOW I'D PROBABLY START DREAMING ABOUT MISSING AN IMPORTANT MEETING.
BRIGHT GLAD MORNING, DAWN CHORUS TWITTER ♫, TWEET, SUN'S RAYS STREAMING IN, JAMES GALWAY FLUTE ETC...
I NEVER THOUGHT I'D SEE THE DAY WHEN I'D LOOK FORWARD TO BREAKFAST T.V.!
CLICK
NNNN
COMING UP NEXT, YET ANOTHER LOOK AT THE WEATHER, THEN THIS WEEKS MOVIE AWARDS FOLLOWED BY A LOOK AT THIS MORNING'S PAPERS WITH PRINCESS MICHAEL OF KENT...

OKAY – THIS NEXT ONE'S ABOUT LIVING ON THE EDGE AND IT'S RIDDLED WITH TUNEFUL SELF-PITY...
A fashion favourite in its own right, this cowboy hat is very practical, too. In showerproof polyester/cotton with a wide protective brim. Available in leaf green, navy or beige.
RECORD YOUR OWN VOICE ON
VIDEO
MINS FOR £5
ONLY ONE BUSKER AT A TIME
BSOLUTELY NO
RY ICE, LASERS
WIND MACHINES
ALLOWED
HURRY UP, CHUM, – I'VE GOT A LOVER'S FAREWELL TO RENDER.
VIDEO

DESIGN FOR LIVING

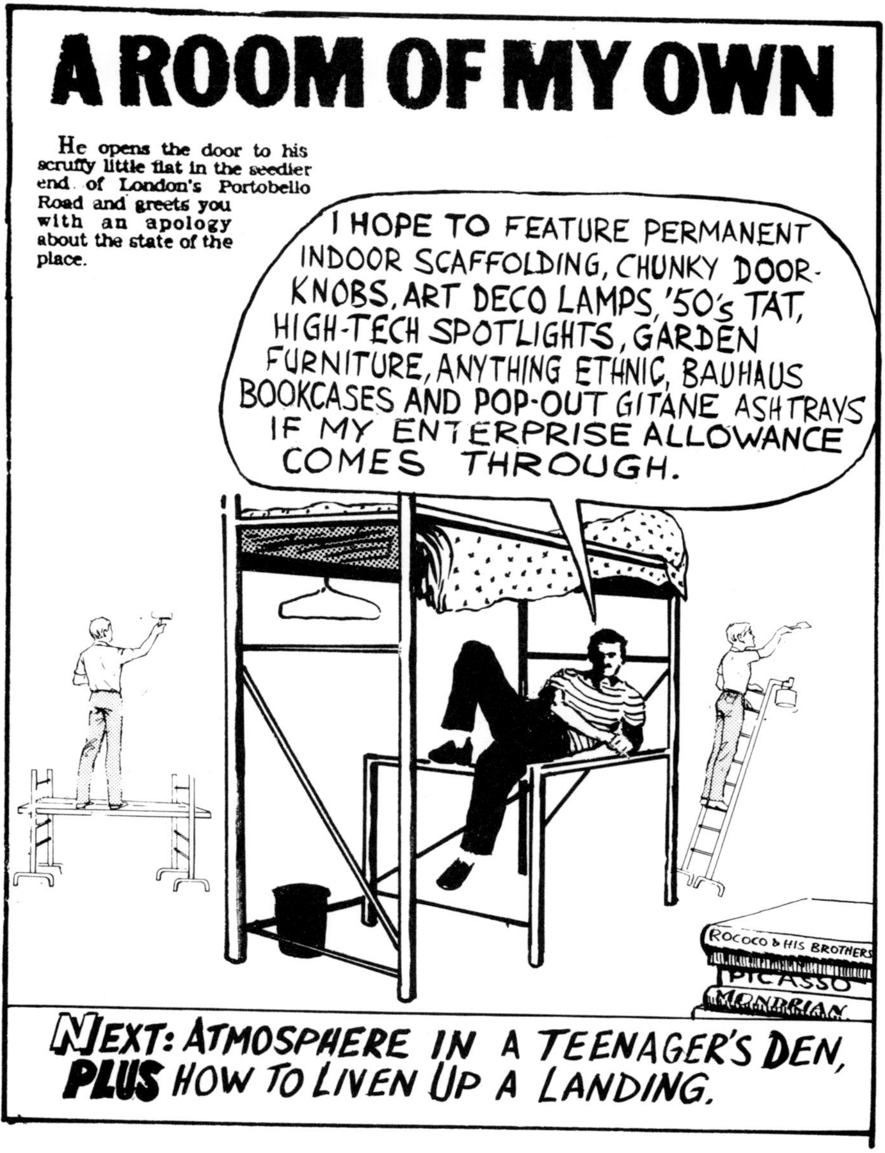

A ROOM OF MY OWN
He opens the door to his scruffy little flat in the seedier end of London's Portobello Road and greets you with an apology about the state of the place.
I HOPE TO FEATURE PERMANENT INDOOR SCAFFOLDING, CHUNKY DOOR-KNOBS, ART DECO LAMPS, '50's TAT, HIGH-TECH SPOTLIGHTS, GARDEN FURNITURE, ANYTHING ETHNIC, BAUHAUS BOOKCASES AND POP-OUT GITANE ASHTRAYS IF MY ENTERPRISE ALLOWANCE COMES THROUGH.
ROCOCO & HIS BROTHERS
PICASSO
MONDRIAN
NEXT: ATMOSPHERE IN A TEENAGER'S DEN, PLUS HOW TO LIVEN UP A LANDING.

REAL LIFE LIBRARY
No.4: PROBLEMS OF OWNERSHIP.
Written by the 'father' of telephone selling
LET'S FACE IT– I'LL NEVER GET PICKED FOR THE "ROOM OF MY OWN" SERIES, SO WHY DON'T I JUNK HALF THIS CRAP? (EXIT RIGHT.)
H. HODGKIN
ROTEL
TIME TO BREAK THE PACKAGE TOUR OF HABIT! I CAN REMEMBER WHEN I COULD FIT ALL MY WORLDLY GOODS INTO ONE SUITCASE!
COO! IT'S THAT GUY WITH THE OUT-OF-DATE TUXEDO!
THATS DECIDED THEN! I'LL GET OUT THE GESTETNER AND RUN OFF SOME LEAFLETS.
HOUSE SALE
EVERYTHING MUST GO! PRICES SLASHED!
I GOT A BIT BOGGED DOWN WITH THE DETAILS...
?
–PERHAPS I'D BETTER HANG ON TO THESE IN CASE I EVER OPEN A SECOND-HAND RECORD SHOP IN BRIGHTON.
Albums
JOE
The MAGIC of
Never Mind the Bollocks
EVE BOSWELL Greatest Hits!
Eagles Half Dead at Hammersmith Odeon
STEVIE WONDER
Crosby, Stills

HMM... NEVER DID GET TO GRIPS WITH STRUCTURAL ANTHRO-POLOGY, THE POST-FREUDIANS, BIOSPHERES OR MODERN FEMINIST ESSAYS — I'LL FILE THEM UNDER 'DECISIONS PENDING.'
SHALL I BUNG THE CASTENEDAS IN THE PARAPSYCHOLOGY BOX?
CLAN→
GENERATION X
BOOKS
NO — I CAN'T PART WITH MY SUEDETTE CLOGS... I WORE THEM ON MY FIRST DATE!
BRONZE MEDAL.
MAYBE YOU COULD WEAR THEM TO A BAD TASTE PARTY.
THERE MUST BE SOMETHING ELSE I DON'T WANT TO KEEP.
...AH, FANCY FINDING MY 1979 DIARY UNDER THE CAT TRAY.
UNFORTUNATELY THIS JOB DOESN'T CARRY A PENSION.
I GUESS I'M THE ANAL RETENTIVE TYPE.
WELL, SO FAR YOU'VE GOT A PLASTIC GUITAR, 10 LAMPSHADES, A STAMP ALBUM, TWO SWEATERS AND A COMPLETE SET OF "MAN, MYTH AND MAGIC."
LATER, DOWN AT THE CAFE...
BINGO!
MAYBE I'LL SHAVE MY MOUSTACHE OFF INSTEAD.
GOD! YOU GEMINIS ARE SO INDECISIVE!
BEANS ON TWO TOASTS!
NEXT: HOW TO BECOME A PYRAMID SALESPERSON WITHOUT VISITING EGYPT. + £1M. GAME.

NEXT MORNING...
NO-ONE EVER WRITES TO ME ANY MORE, -EXCEPT MY BANK MANAGER.
HIS 'N' HERS SARONG
WHAT'S THIS? IT SAYS, "OPEN IMMEDIATELY!" GREAT SCOTT — IT'S A SPECIAL INTRODUCTORY OFFER!
ALPHABET TIE
ALL BRAN
All the facts about: Bowel Cancer Piles
IMPOR
Congratulations, Mr. P.Z.Hux
have personally been selected from
the phone book, Mr. P.Z.Huxtable to
take part in our £5,000,000 yes Mr.
P.Z.Huxtable ,£5,000,000 competition.
You have already won a prize, Mr.
P.Z.Huxtable which will shortly be
lowered into your back garden by
helicopter
WITHOUT FURTHER OBLIGATION, I COULD WIN £65,000 AND A TRIP TO FARAWAY PLACES ON THE Q.E.2 WITH MY OWN COFFEE PERCOLATOR!
WHAT NEXT? DECK QUOITS OR A DIAQUARI BINGE?
MEN'S TRAVEL KIT
DREAM SEQUENCE
...THIS ONE SAYS A SMOOTH, DE LUXE SALOON CAR WITH AN INSULATED PICNIC BAG COULD SOON BE GLIDING UP TO MY TOP-FLOOR FLAT!
SHALL WE TAKE A SPIN ROUND TO THE SUPERMARKET?
LADIES CALCULATOR WALLET

HEY—THIS LOOKS GOOD... "FASHIONABLE CLOTHES AT KNOCK-DOWN PRICES"... I MIGHT BE ALLOWED INTO THE CAMDEN PALACE AT LAST!
HI! CAN I COME IN TO HIP-HOP AWHILE?
PIERRE CARDIN HIP WALLET
MMM... WONDERFUL!
—OR I COULD START A "PROFITABLE SIDELINE BUSINESS BY TELEPHONE WITHOUT KNOCKING MYSELF OUT"....(PITY I'VE BEEN DISCONNECTED)
AH, HELLO... CAN I INTEREST YOU IN SOME DIRT CHEAP BRITISH TELECOM SHARES?
NAVIGATORS PAPERWEIGHT
—THEN IN MY SPARE TIME I CAN LOLL ABOUT WITH "A THICK AND GLOSSY BOOK PLUS ANY 3 OTHERS IN HAND-TOOLED LEATHER FINISH COMPLETE WITH A SUPERB COPPER-ETCHED PORTRAIT OF THE AUTHOR."
DID YOU KNOW THAT AMERICAN RESEARCHERS HAVE DEVELOPED A TELEPHONE LINK WITH THE DEAD?
AMAZING FACTS
GOLD PLATED BOOKMARK
HAND OF FATE
—TROUBLE IS, THEY'RE ALL FOR PEOPLE WHO LEFT HERE YEARS AGO.
I CAN'T EVEN MAKE IT ONTO A COMPUTER!
TELESCOPIC TIE RACK
FREE
OPEN
POST WITHIN 14 DAYS FOR THE CHANCE £15,000 BONUS
OH NO! —NOT ANOTHER CHAIN LETTER!

A LAVISH SPREAD

TRAVEL AGENT
...YES, I THINK YOU'LL ENJOY IT THERE.... PUT YOUR FEET UP... GIVE THE OLD BRAIN-CELLS A REST.... OF COURSE, WE MUST RECOGNISE THAT WE CAN NEVER ACHIEVE TOTAL TRANQUILITY.... AS PRODUCTS OF TIME, WE CAN NEVER FIND THAT WHICH IS TIMELESS!
GREAT! WHAT'S THE NIGHT-LIFE LIKE?
DO YOU HAVE ANY VACANCIES IN TORQUAY? THE I CHING SAID I SHOULD MOVE TO THE SOUTH-WEST.
I'LL BE ABLE TO TRY OUT MY NEW INSECT REPELLENT.
CLOSED
ENQUIRIES
The Magic of GREECE
WALLY'S COACH TOURS
*Scenic Trips.
*Nightly Piss-ups.

The Mirror Phase

TIGHT WAISTBANDS DON'T MAKE IT...
IS THIS MIDDLE-AGE SPREAD OR THE POST-LAUNDERETTE SYNDROME?
THOU, O YOUTH ART THE TUBBIEST OF THEM ALL.
Brut
Frigidaire
LATE NIGHT SNACK COMPARTMENT

MY HANDS ARE SHAKING AND MY KNEES ARE WEAK, DOC... I CAN'T SEEM TO STAND ON MY OWN TWO FEET...
HMMM.... SOUNDS TO ME AS IF YOU'RE ALL SHOOK UP.
DOC. MARTEN
A present from Sidmouth
OLD TUMOURS ETC

PRISONER OF GENDER
A BEDTIME STORY.
TINA-SO GOOD TO SEE A FRIENDLY FACE...LISTEN, CAN I HARANGUE YOU WITH MY VERSION OF EVENTS—?
WELL ACTUALLY BRIAN I'M ALREADY LATE FOR MY CREATIVE WRITING CLASS.
....YOU SEE, I NEVER WANTED TO TIE HER DOWN, YEAH? I ALWAYS GAVE HER HER FREEDOM BUT SHE WAS AFRAID TO RISK— ...I'M NOT BORING YOU, AM I.?
NO, NO REALLY, —I'M JUST MEDITATING.
PHOTOS OF HARRY
HOW TO BUILD A SHED
IT WAS ONLY WHEN I WENT AWAY THAT SHE REALISED HER STRENGTH; —OF COURSE, SHE HAD A TOUGH CHILDHOOD...
I JUST DON'T BELIEVE THIS GUY. IS THIS A WIND-UP?
...BUT NOW, I SUPPOSE, I FEEL DISAPPOINTED THAT I WON'T BE AROUND TO BE PART OF HER CHANGE, YEAH? —SHE WAS ON THE BRINK OF SOMETHING SPECIAL— IT WOULD'VE BEEN A CHALLENGE!
CONDESCENDING PRAT!
...STILL, WITH US IT'S A QUESTION OF LOSING OURSELVES, HOPEFULLY TO ARRIVE AT A TOTALLY NEW STARTING POINT.
WHAT'S HAPPENED THEN? ARE YOU SPLITTING UP?
-SORT OF —— SHE'S TEMPORARILY BUGGERED OFF WITH SOMEONE ELSE.
WELL I'M BLOWED.
YES, HARD TO BELIEVE ISN'T IT?
COMPREHENSION TEST:
1. ACCOUNT FOR BRIAN'S BEING GIVEN THE BUM'S RUSH.
2. IMAGINE YOU ARE A CAT WAITING TO BE FED. DESCRIBE YOUR THOUGHTS.
2 HOURS ALLOWED.

IT'S ALMOST TOMORROW
A POWERFUL AND FORTHRIGHT SETTING OF THIS DRAMATIC POEM, PERFORMED HERE IN ENGLISH TRANSLATION WITH A PARALLEL ENACTMENT OF THE CLASSICAL STORY BY SHADOW PUPPETS.
SOMEWHERE IN 1985...
BASICALLY I'VE JUST GOT TO RESTRUCTURE MY LIFE...
WHY? HAVE YOU MISLAID YOUR FILOFAX ?
LET ME KNOW WHEN YOU'RE READY TO TAKE A LETTER, BY THE WAY.
BLEEP-BLEEP
"I'LL START BY GETTING MY ACT TOGETHER..."
BRAN CITY WHOLEFOODS
-WONDERFUL... I'LL GIVE YOU THE PHONE NUMBER OF MY ACUPUNCTURIST.
YAH - I'VE GIVEN UP MEAT, CHEESE, EGGS, CUT DOWN ON WINE AND DOPE AND STARTED DOING WORK-OUTS.
"...BE MORE SELF-CONFIDENT..."
WHEN'S YOUR PROFILE APPEARING ON THE 'SOUTH BANK SHOW'?
DEUCE!
WELL, I HAVEN'T ACTUALLY WRITTEN ANY OF THE TRILOGY YET... I'M STILL READING AROUND THE SUBJECT.
"-TRAVEL ON IMPULSE..."
SCOOP!... "I FOLLOW THE RUCKSACK TRAIL".
TWA
DING-DONG... WILL THE BEARDED MAN OF MYSTERY PLEASE PHONE HIS OFFICE TO EXPLAIN HIS ABSENCE.
GATE 10
DING-DONG. ALL THOSE HAVING RELATIVES AND FRIENDS ON FLIGHT 1203...
"FULFILL ROMANTIC INCLINATIONS..."
MMM... THE COMPUTER DIDN'T STIPULATE ARABLE INTERESTS!
I'M NOT MUCH FOR PRETTY SPEECHES - BUT HOW ABOUT GETTING MARRIED AFTER HAY-MAKING ?
RUPERT BEAR COUNTRY
FAST FORWARD...
BUT YOU SAID ALL THIS LAST YEAR - AND THE YEAR BEFORE THAT!
I KNOW... IT'S AN ETERNAL RECURRENCE... NOW THAT'S ANOTHER THING I'M GOING TO GET INTO...
-TO BE CONTINUED IN 1986...

LOOK-I'M SORRY I CALLED YOU WOODY ALLEN WITHOUT THE SENSE OF HUMOUR, OKAY?
BUT YOU KNOW HOW SENSITIVE I CAN BE.
16 PINTS A NIGHT
Meat Loaf

AH, IT'S GOOD TO BE ON ANOTHER LEISURELY VOYAGE UP THAT MYTHICAL RIVER OF THE ***SELF***...
SHIFT YOUR FEET, –I NEED TO HOOVER UNDER THERE.
Park Drive
Selected Poems.
by
Tristan Blade.
LOST HORIZONS

I JUST WANT TO SHUT OUT THE WORLD AND LOSE MYSELF IN YOU, BABE.
THAT'S VERY SWEET OF YOU.
NOT ANOTHER EMOTIONALLY DEPENDENT BLOKE LOOKING FOR A MOTHER!

HELL IS MY DESTINATION!
HE WAS ALWAYS TRAVELLING... NEVER ARRIVING...
-JUST LIKE TO REMIND PASSENGERS THAT THE BAR AND BUFFET IS STILL OPEN FOR THE SALE OF ALCCHOLIC AND NON-ALCOHOLIC BEVERAGES, TEA, COFFEE, SANDWICHES TOASTED SANDWICHES HOT & COLD SNACKS AND THE ALL-DAY BREAKFAST THANKYOU.
HERE I AM - NEARLY 30 AND STILL CAN'T DECIDE WHETHER TO COMB MY HAIR BACKWARDS OR FORWARDS!
SORRY, YOUR TICKET'S NOT VALID ON THIS TRAIN ON FRIDAYS.

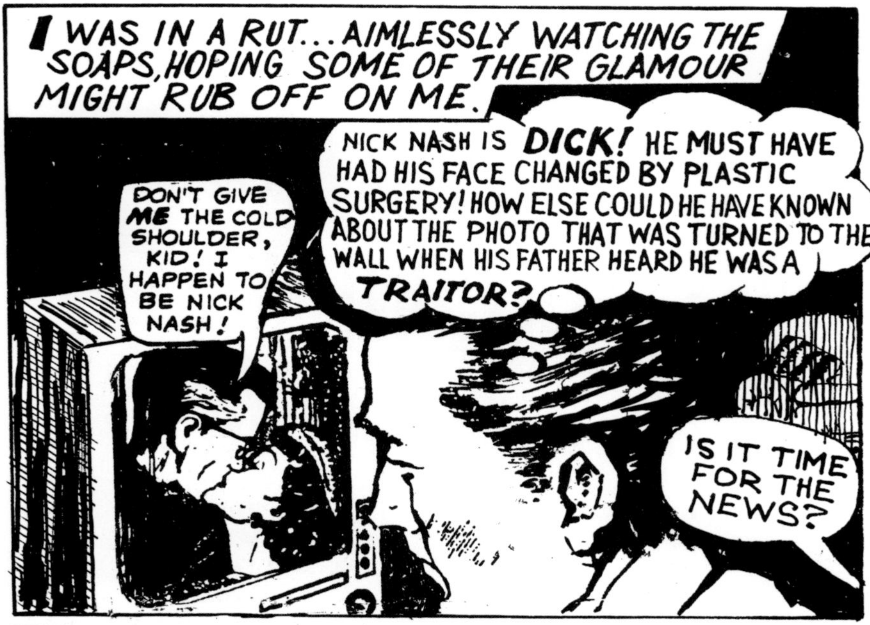

*POETIC T.V. LICENCE.

EVERYONE WAS VERY SUPPORTIVE BUT I COULD TELL I WAS BORING THEM...
...AND THEN WHAT?
Bread
Milk
Eggs
NO SALE
NO - I NEEDED A SABBATICAL; SO I WENT THROUGH MY ADDRESS BOOK...
THINK OF IT, MATE, -JUST LIKE THE OLD DAYS- YOU AND ME, STUCK FOR HOURS AT THE HAMMERSMITH FLY-OVER! WHADDYA SAY?

BUT ROY WAS ON A READING BINGE...
ALEX WON'T BE TOO HAPPY WITH THAT SHOT - HE'S PUT THE CUE CLEAN THROUGH THE BAIZE!
MEMORY IS A VERSION OF THE PAST THAT WAS NEVER PRESENT, BAZ....LOOK, -TALK TO YOU LATER-O.K?
NICK WAS AWAY DOING CABARET UP NORTH...
I'D LIKE TO DEDICATE THIS NEXT SONG TO OUR COMMUNITY POLICEMAN...HE'S SO HIP-HE GOES DANCING EVERY NIGHT AND THE KIDS ALL CALL HIM THE DISCO TEC!
Vexations

AND KEITH WAS IN CONFERENCE WITH HIS COMMISSIONING EDITOR...
I STILL THINK IT'S A CLUMSY DEVICE INTRODUCING A MARXIST BEST MAN INTO THE WEDDING RECEPTION SCENE.
CIGAR
USED CAR
THERE YOU GO AGAIN; —YOU MEDIA PEOPLE WANT EVERYTHING WRAPPED UP SAFE AND COSY, ANYTHING CONTRA-VERSIAL THREATENS YOUR **CONSENSUS**!
AT FIRST, PRU SEEMED KEEN... BUT THEN HER CAT GOT ILL.
A SOUL SAFARI, YOU SAY? SOUNDS FUN... WE COULD MAKE A **ROAD MOVIE**!
WHAT ROTTEN LUCK! YOU MUST GO ALONE!
I CAN'T LEAVE YOU LIKE THIS.
MIEAOU!
PILLS

ROGER, I KNEW, WOULD BE ON THE THRESHOLD OF A NEW DAWN...
QUICK! - GET THE FLASKS! - I THINK I'VE SEEN INTO THE FUTURE!
SHALL I PHONE FOR THE BRIGADIER AND ARRANGE THE PULP PAPERBACK RIGHTS, PROFESSOR?
LAB
MAXW HOUS

SO IN THE END I DECIDED TO GO IT ALONE: I CALLED BY THE LOCAL UNISEX PARLOUR TO GET SPRUCED UP.
SPECIAL OFFER 100% HUMAN HAIR
WIGLETS
FITS ANY HEAD SIZE. IMPROVES MEMORY POWERS INSTANTLY. NO PREVIOUS EXISTENCE NECESSARY.
ONLY 4.99P
BARBED WIRE LOOK
NASA
I'LL JUST LOP OFF A FEW CLUMPS HERE AND THERE, SHALL I? DO YOU REQUIRE - AHEM - ANYTHING FOR THE WEEKEND, SIR?
-GOT ANY OLD RECORDS YOU DON'T WANT? I'M GOING AWAY...

AND SO, TWO WEEKS LATER...
I WONDER HOW I'LL COPE WITH THE LONELINESS?
THE LAUGHING POLICEMAN

THE POPULAR ARTS

I DON'T BOTHER TO WATER THIS PLANT - I JUST GIVE IT BACH AND BEETHOVEN.
I PLAYED SOME AC/DC TO MY SPIDER-PLANT - BLOODY THING KEELED OVER!
BILL BRANDT EFFECT

He is an authority on animals and has a rare talent for capturing them authentically yet artistically.
He is a perfectionist who sets the very highest standards and insists on inspecting each print himself.
HERE – THIS IS NOT A REPRESENTATION OF REALITY BUT THE REALITY OF THAT REPRESENTATION.... ... IT'S ALSO BLURRED.
HOW COME I ALWAYS GET THE DUFF PARTS?
HAVE YOUR PHOTO TAKEN WITH 'PEDRO' THE MONKEY
PRINTS READY WHILE-U-WAIT
PROP: MIKE LEGGETT
50p

ONE OF THE SHORTEST STORIES EVER TOLD!
Listen to the Cadenza of Confusion in the
CONCERTO OF CRIME!
THE DETECTIVE NOVEL OF MANNERS WITH A HAPPY ENDING!
I WAS JUST AN ORDINARY SOCIOLOGIST UNTIL...
TIN PAN ALLEY W.1
IT SAYS HERE YOU CAN BE A TOP-FLIGHT PIANIST IN 7 DAYS; NO MUSICAL EXPERIENCE NECESSARY!
SIDESADDLE TOPS CHARTS
NME
WEEDON HEAD READING
NEXT DAY....
—YES, YOU SHOULD GET PLENTY OF INSPIRATION IN THAT TITFER, SIR: DEBUSSY WORE IT FOR ALL HIS MATURE COMPOSITIONS!
I SEEK TO BE THE VAN GOGH OF THE IVORIES. —I'LL TAKE IT!
BUT IT WAS A STING...
I WANT MY MONEY BACK, — I'VE TURNED INTO D.H. LAWRENCE!
OPEN
AH YES, THEN YOU'LL BE WANTING OUR LITERATURE SECTION, SIR.
BUT, EVER THE PRAGMATIST, I SIMPLY GOT MY AGENT TO MAKE THE SWITCH FROM CONCERTS TO SERIALISATION RIGHTS.
WHY ARE YOU TELLING ME ALL THIS, INSPECTOR?
TURF
EITHER TRACE THE IMPACT OF THE PANAMA HAT ON POST-WAR CRIME STATISTICS,
OR WRITE A TWELVE VOLUME NOVEL IN WHICH NOTHING HAPPENS.

Poet in Residence.
...THIS NEXT ONE'S ABOUT OUR MUCH-LOVED FAMILY CAT AND THE TRAGEDY THAT BEFELL IT ONE DAY WHILE WE WEREN'T THERE – THE BOYS WERE AWAY AT SCHOOL, MY WIFE WAS TRAVELLING IN MEXICO AND I WAS UP IN TOWN WITH MY PUBLISHER; – IT STARVED TO DEATH. AHEM..."O SIMPLE CREATURE OF THE WILD, STALKING THE BRITTLE GRASSES IN NIGHTLY STEALTH....."
Z-Z-Z-Z-Z-Z-Z

The Film Society
Starting on Friday 13th there will be a series of poorly attended films followed by a pricey round of drinks in the pub opposite.
I CAN ENVISAGE A TIME WHEN THERE WILL BE NO MORE CINEMA - JUST A DISCUSSION OVER A PINT LATER.
WE HAVE TO BROADEN OUR APPEAL...
...BUT NOT AT THE EXPENSE OF THE SOCIAL ASPECT. WHO'S IS THE BITTER?

WE COME NOW TO THE FINAL WORK IN OUR LUNCHTIME RECITAL OF DIEGO RODRIGUES' "SEVEN MEDITATIONS ON THE THEME OF DEATH", GIVEN BY THE RUE MORGUE QUARTET. COMPOSED IN SONATA FORM, THE REMOTE HARMONIES AND GLACIAL TEXTURES OF THIS PIECE EVOKE FEELINGS OF UTTER DESOLATION. IT'S ENTITLED "OBLIVION" AND FEATURES JUAN FERNANDEZ ON WASHBOARD..... OKAY, TAKE IT AWAY, BOYS.
ON AIR
BBC

...AT 7.30, MORE COMEDY FROM THE APARTMENT-SHARING DIVORCEES, THEN AT 8'O'CLOCK, A SPECIAL TRIBUTE TO A VERY SPECIAL LADY, H.M. THE QUEEN MOTHER. THEN, FOLLOWING THE NEWS, ANOTHER IN OUR SHORT SEASON OF THROAT-CLUTCHERS DIRECTED BY AND STARRING THE RICH AND TALENTLESS SON OF A TV-MOVIE HAM, FULL OF VIOLENCE AND SPURIOUS SENTIMENT. FINALLY, THERE'S SOME SERIOUS, DIFFICULT, VAGUELY RADICAL STUFF THAT YOU'LL BE TOO WIPED OUT TO TAKE IN...
T.V. DINNER
NEXT TIME I BABYSIT I MUST BRING A GOOD BOOK.

—DON'T THINK I COULD HANDLE ANOTHER PRAWN BIRIANI TONIGHT. . . I THINK I'LL JUST GRAB A COUPLE OF FISH-CAKES ON THE WAY HOME.
SIZZLE! CRASH! THUD!
OOYAH OOYAH!
HI.
HONK! SQUEAL!
UGH! UNNGH!
LORD GOWRIE HAIRSTYLE
PLINK! PLONK!
PLUNK! PLUNK!

I WANT IT TO CONFRONT ALL THE ISSUES CONCERNING THE **SOCIAL PRODUCTION OF MEANING.**
TELL ME MORE... —LOOK, SHALL I ORDER SOME CHIPS WHILE WE'RE WAITING?
GOLLY! I SAW THEM ON CHANNEL FOUR LAST WEEK!
WELL, I'VE BEEN LOOKING AT SOME SCRIPTS.. BUT CURRENTLY I'M MODELLING A MACHINE THAT REMOVES CHEWING GUM FROM CARPETS.
BAR
SCRIPT

I DATED A FILM BUFF
PRODUCED BY DAVID PUTTNAM
AN INTERESTING DRAMATISATION OF AN EVERYDAY EVENT.
FREE! B.A.F.T.A. AWARD WITH EVERY 5 LITRES OF SHELL MULTGRADE OIL.
ACTUALLY, I FOUND IT A COMPELLING ESSAY ON NATURE, ARTICULATED IN A SELF-REFLEXIVE MANNER THAT NEATLY SIDE-STEPPED THE PITFALLS OF FEY ROMANTICISM...
"EMOTION RIPPED BARE"
NOW ALL OVER LONDON
WAY OUT
WHAT DID YOU THINK OF THE MOVIE?
WHY NOT TRY A JUMBO HOTDOG?
OUTSIDE, I REALISED I HAD STARTED SOMETHING THAT WOULD BE VERY HARD TO STOP.
UH-HUH... SHALL WE DROP INTO THE WAG CLUB?
...BY MEANS OF A DENSELY PATTERNED PLOT WHICH HELD ITS AMBIGUITIES IN EXCRUCIATINGLY-ER-NEUTRAL TENSION.
AS FOR THE BEAUTIFULLY PHOTOGRAPHED SLOW-MOTION SCENES, GIVEN DIGNITY BY THE HAUNTING LEITMOTIF OF THE MOUTH-ORGAN, I-ER...
LOOK—CAN'T WE JUST DANCE?
I'M IN VINYL REPAIR..
HOW MUCH ARE YOUR MARGUERITES?
LATER, AT THE ALL-NIGHT CAFE, HIS HAND RESTED ON MINE...
...IN SHORT, IT'S A FILM THAT WILL STAY WITH ME LONG AFTER I'VE LEFT THE CINEMA... ...HOW ABOUT YOU?
UNFORTUNATELY I COULDN'T SEE MUCH BECAUSE OF THE COUPLE SNOGGING IN FRONT OF US.
EITHER: MAKE A FILM WITHOUT NATASSIA KINSKI IN IT OR: GIVE EXAMPLES OF RECENT WORK IN WHICH THE SIGNIFIER HAS BEEN FOREGROUNDED.
FIN

MEN ABOUT TOWN

PAGES OF HEAD-TURNING FASHION

1. THE GREAT TALKER.

2. THE LADS

DARTS
TONIGHT
SNAKEBITE ARMS
-V-
WHITE LION
TEAMS
BAGGY SHORT-SLEEVED SHINY SHIRTS ONLY PLEASE
OF COURSE, I'M ONLY A SOCIAL DRINKER MYSELF.
ME TOO - I FIND IT WORKS LIKE MAGIC TO GIVE YOU ADDED POISE, SELF CONFIDENCE AND GREATER POPULARITY.
FIFTY PINTS OF LAGER PLEASE STUART, AND ONE FOR YOUR GOOD SELF.
Pork Scratchings
Menu
BIFF.

3. THE OVER-ANALYTICAL.

4. rugged reliability

5. THE RECENT CONVERT.

6. THE HUMAN CLICHE.

7. THE DREAMY TYPE.

8. THE TIME-WASTER.

Modern Problems and their Solutions

★ Packed with professional tips and time-saving hints. ★

TROUBLE WITH THE HI·FI
-ONLY GOT IT LAST WEEK!
IT DEPENDS WHICH SIDE OF THE ROOM YOU ARE...OR MAYBE YOU NEED AN EQUALIZER.
IS THE DECK COMPATIBLE?
YOU COULD CEMENT THE SPEAKERS INTO THE WALL.
SQUEAL.....
-HUM.....
...TAXI RADIO....
BZZZ.....
-HISS.....
RUMBLE...
SOUND TRAVELS BETTER THROUGH WATER.. —HAVE YOU TRIED PUTTING THE SPEAKERS IN THE FISHTANK?

Breaking the Ice with New Neighbours
SHOT ENTIRELY ON LOCATION ON AN EXECUTIVE ESTATE USING NON-PROFESSIONAL ACTORS AND OTHER COST-SAVING TACTICS MASQUERADING AS NATURALISM.
RICHARD HOGGART LIVED HERE
NEVER PREJUDGE...
THAT'LL BE THEM NOW - I'LL GET THE DIET-FREE PINACOLADA SIX-PACK FROM THE FREEZER.
I HOPE THEY'RE NOT UPWARDLY MOBILE JOGGERS.
THEME FROM 'NEWSNIGHT' CHIME
SOD IT - I'VE LOST COUNT
SHOW SOME INTEREST..
SO... YOU'RE IN THE MAIL ORDER RACKET EH, ROD?
THAT'S RIGHT, - IT'S STILL JUST ABOUT THE ONLY FIELD WHERE THE, QUOTES, LITTLE GUY, CAN GO NATIONAL OVERNIGHT.
EASE THEM INTO THEIR NEW SURROUNDINGS...
WELL, NOW WE'VE ALL GOT TO KNOW EACH OTHER BETTER, PERHAPS YOU'D LIKE TO SEE OUR SLIDES OF LAST MONTH'S JUMBLE SALE, YEAH?
25ft FLEXIBLE DRAIN CLEANER
IMPENDING GLOOM
?
ER.... - I THINK WE MAY HAVE LEFT THE CHIP PAN ON.
...OR MAYBE YOU'D CARE TO JOIN US IN THE HOT TUB.

THE L-PLATES OF CONTRADICTION
HE WAS READY TO BE MOVIN' N' A-GROOVIN'...
THE DAY OF MY DRIVING TEST ARRIVED... I WAS BURSTING WITH CONFIDENCE...
THIS CRATE HANDLES SURPRISINGLY WELL– DOES IT HAVE DUAL CIRCUIT STEERING, MISERLY FUEL FIGURES AND CLOSE RATIO GEARS TO GIVE SURE-FOOTED CORNERING?
KINDLY CONCENTRATE ON YOUR CLUTCH CO-ORDINATION.
HIGHWAY OF CONSCIOUSNESS
READING
ROUTE 66
BUT, AS USUAL, NAGGING DOUBTS CREPT IN...
MAYBE I'M ONE OF THOSE PEOPLE WHO GO THROUGH LIFE WITHOUT TEST-DRIVING UP A MOTORWAY USING A HOME COMPUTER OR WINNING A FRAME OF SNOOKER.
OKAY, I WANT YOU TO PULL OUT SLOWLY AND GIVE HAND SIGNALS.
THINKING IS THE ONLY
I TRIED TO RATIONALISE MY FEARS..
STILL, CARS JUST CLOG UP CITY CENTRES, POLLUTE THE ENVIRONMENT AND DRAIN RESOURCES*...
..BESIDES, IT'S ANOTHER PRIVATISATION OF EXPERIENCE BEHIND GLASS AND METAL... ANYWAY, I CAN'T AFFORD TO RUN A CAR...
(YAWN) – STOP OVER THERE AND WE'LL DO THE HIGHWAY CODE.
...BUT THEN SHE TOLD ME I'D PASSED!
WILL YOU JOIN A CAR CLUB OR JUST DO THE OCCASIONAL LE MANS?
I THOUGHT I'D START WITH A 'T' REG. DEUX CHEVAUX WHICH I'LL CALL JEAN-LUC...
KAMI-CARS DRIVING SCHOOL
PART 6: HOW TO DRIVE BACKWARDS.
*THIS BUBBLE SPONSORED BY CYCLISTS FOR A CLEAN PLANET

HAUTE CUISINE SANS LE HASSLE
THIS IS JERRY – HE'S BRINGING HIS NEW BOSS HOME FOR SUPPER TONIGHT. WHAT CAN I GIVE HER THAT'S NOT A DULL AND ORDINARY DISH?
TWANG!
IT'S 8·23 HERE ON RADIO ONE.. HAVE A NICE DAY IF YOU'RE JUST OFF TO WORK OF EVEN IF YOU'RE JUST STAYING AT HOME AFTER ALL IT'S A FULL-TIME JOB BEING A HOUSEWIFE THESE DAYS BURBLE BURBLE...
PORRIDGE
LUCKILY, BETTY POPPED ROUND TO BORROW A CUP OF SUGAR...
...IF I WERE YOU, I'D CHOOSE ANY THREE OF THE FOLLOWING: Mussels "Poulette" Fried Rice Croquettes Timbale of Sweetbreads and Macaroni Hungarian Cherry Soup Dandelion and Bacon Salad Tangerine Stuffing Diplomat Pudding Steak and Kidney steamed within a Pastry Chicken Livers with Cucumbers Blueberry Muffins Banana Bread Coffee Truffles Provençal Pizza French Moussaka with Watercress Mushroom Caps Stuffed and Gratineed Deep-Fried Veal with a Cheese-and-Crumb Crust York Ham Braised in Madeira....
OXFA
...OR YOU COULD DO Pear Upside-Down Tart Meringue Cake Beef and Onions in Beer Cheese and Egg Custard Butterscotch Ice Cream Sauce Sole in Red Wine, . –THAT'S ALWAYS NICE..
–BUT IN THE END THERE WASN'T TIME, SO I SETTLED FOR SOMETHING MORE TRADITIONAL...
MMM.... SLAP-UP FEED THIS – YOU'VE CERTAINLY LANDED THAT JOB IN OVERSEAS SALES, JERRY!
ELKIE BROOKS
PRIDE
LEAVE A LITTLE ROOM FOR THE SPOTTED DICK.

THROWING A PARTY
REMEMBER TO PLAN AHEAD...
SHALL WE OPEN WITH SLOW SOUL OR REGGAE AND BUILD TO A CRESCENDO OF AFRICAN HI-LIFE?
SCRATCH VIDEO
ANYTHING, AS LONG AS IT'S CRUCIAL.
ALWAYS DO THE ROUNDS...
ENJOYING YOURSELVES? -EXCUSE ME....I MUST CIRCULATE.
YES, THIS IS THE BEST DO WE'VE GATE-CRASHED ALL EVENING.
THE JELLY IS MAGNIFICENT!
HI - I DON'T WANT TO TALK SHOP, BUT DIDN'T I SEE YOU AT THE LABOUR PARTY CONFERENCE?
Help yourself to one of the lovely eggy poppy seed rolls and dig in to the substantial sweetcorn chowder thick with bacon and onion. Less hearty eaters could start with attractive oriental salad (bean shoots, red and green peppers, palm and artichoke hearts) or perhaps tomato and onion, or crudites.
AND, AS THE PUBS EMPTY, BE PREPARED FOR EXIGENCIES...
HEY THE NEIGHBOURS JUST RANG TO COMPLAIN ABOUT THE NOISE!
HI-ENJOYING YOURSELVES?
HAVEN'T YOU GOT ANY DISCO-FUNK? -NOBODY'S BREAK-DANCING!
OH GOD... NEVER AGAIN GOD... URRGH! (SPLATTER)
HOW MUCH LONGER IS HE GOING TO BE IN THERE?
WE'RE OUT OF WINE - SHALL I ORGANISE A WHIP-ROUND?
THEN AFTERWARDS ALLOW YOURSELVES A FEW MOMENTS TO WIND DOWN....
MORE OR LESS....THERE'S JUST THAT BLOKE THAT NOBODY KNEW WHO'S TANKED UP AND CRASHED OUT ON OUR BED.
WELL, THAT WENT REASONABLY OKAY. HAS EVERYONE GONE HOME?
SORRY, I THINK I LEFT MY CONTACT LENSES IN THE BATHROOM.

HANDLING THE SUPERSALESPERSON
DING DONG
ALLOW HIM/HER HIS/HER SAY...
..YOU SEE GEORGE - MAY I CALL YOU GEORGE?.. ..I LOVE THESE PRODUCTS AND SO WILL YOU: THEY LITERALLY SELL THEMSELVES...OUR CALIFORNIAN AGENT JUST MADE $125,000, YET 3 YEARS AGO HE WAS A BANKRUPT ESTATE AGENT, FORCED TO SELL BOTH HIS T.V. SETS TO RAISE THE CO-LATERAL!
Porch Lantern 9.99
AT LEAST IT'S NOT ANOTHER MORI OPINION POLL.
SALES RAP
...ASK POLITE QUESTIONS EVERY HOUR OR SO...
SO THERE'S NO LINK-UP WITH DOUBLE-GLAZING OR BILLY GRAHAM... AND THE STUFF'S NON-NUCLEAR YOU RECKON?
-GUARANTEED SAFE FOR THE OZONE LAYER GEORGE...SO... YOU'RE INTERESTED? - FINE... WORK FROM HOME... ELIMINATE TRAFFIC WARDENS. GO FOR IT! CHANGE YOUR LIFE FOR THE REST OF YOUR LIFE!!
SCRIPT
-THEN THROW IN THE SPANNER...
- FUNNY YOU SHOULD SAY THAT - THE WIFE'S JUST WON A MILLION QUID ON THE BINGO.
Munch
THERE MUST BE A CORRECT REPLY TO THAT.
AUTO CUE
YAWN

Work, Leisure and the Family, Vol.4:

AHEM...THIS IS JUST LIKE "KRAPP'S LAST TAPE"... ....NO, I SAY THAT EVERY YEAR........I JUST WANT TO BE-ER-SPONTANEOUS.. -NOT TRY TO ADDRESS AN AUDIENCE....THERE IS ALWAYS THE DESIRE TO RETURN TO ZERO... ER.......THIS IS ME OF NOW SPEAKING TO THE ME OF THEN...
HAPPY BIRTHDAY DAD
GRUNDIG
WHO ARE YOU TALKING TO DEAR?

WHAT DID WE DO AT PLAYSCHOOL TODAY?
NOT MUCH... WE JUST BROKE DOWN CONCEPTUAL APPREHENSIONS AND BUILT AN ATMOSPHERE OF MUTUAL TRUST INSIDE WHICH WE COULD BE CREATIVE WITHIN THE CONTEXT OF MUSICAL EXPLORATION, DANCE AND DRAMA SKILLS WHICH MAY BE OBSCURED BY SOCIAL PROCESSING.
TOMORROW WE'RE GOING ON A TRIP TO CHESSINGTON ZOO.

IT WAS MOTHER'S DAY AND I WAS
HOMEWARD BOUND
JILL'S HUSBAND WILL BE COMING, SO TRY TO BE NON-CONTROVERSIAL.
DON'T WORRY MUM. I'LL STICK TO SAFE TOPICS.
"A VISIT TO THE PARENTAL HOME... I SELECTED SOME READING MATTER TO TAKE MY MIND OFF THE COMING ORDEAL..."
BUFFET
..ONLY THROUGH SUCH INTERVENTIONS CAN WE BEGIN TO BUILD A RANK AND FILE, REVO-LUTIONARY ALTERNATIVE TO THE BUREAUCRATIC APPROACH OF THE LABOUR PARTY, YOU SEE.
FINE – GIVE ME TEN COPIES FOR THE JOURNEY.
"THE OMENS WEREN'T TOO GOOD."
BY GOD, THESE JAPANESE KNOW THEIR PHOTOCOPIERS DON'T THEY? MIND YOU, THEY DON'T HAVE THE UNION PROBLEMS, DO THEY?
SHUT YOUR GOB!
YOU MUST EXCUSE ME – I THINK I'LL GO AND TRY THE ALL-DAY BREAKFAST!
Conference News:
Police Praise The Thin Blue Line
SO – THIS WAS JILL'S HUSBAND.. AT FIRST HE WAS FAIRLY LOW KEY..."
IN MY OPINION IT'S YOU CRYPTO-HUMANISTS WHO ARE UNDERMINING EDUCATIONAL STANDARDS IN THIS COUNTRY – I SUPPOSE YOU TAKE THEM ALL ON SAVE THE G.L.C. AND JOB MARCHES!
NORMAN TEBBIT LOOK
WELL, I DO FAVOUR A BROAD-BASED CURRICULUM. BUT WHAT DO YOU THINK OF THE TOUR SIDE.... THEY SHOULD'VE TAKEN RANDALL, DON'T YOU THINK?
WHY CAN'T I HAVE RIGHT ON IN-LAWS LIKE EVERYONE ELSE?
MMM – YES, YOU SEE, THE WEEKENDS ARE THE ONLY TIME I GET TO DO THE GARDENING..
BURBLE
CLINK!
"I TRIED TO STEER THE CONVERSATION AWAY BUT HE KEPT ON NIGGLING..."
– YOU TELL THEM MAGGIE!.... YOU SEE – SHE KNOWS HOW TO GET THE MESSAGE ACROSS. I IMAGINE YOUR CROWD LOUNGE ABOUT WATCHING CHANNEL 4 ALL EVENING!
...AND THEY SHOULD SEND THOSE SCRUFFY WOMEN BACK HOME TO LOOK AFTER THEIR CHILDREN! BUT OF COURSE, YOU'RE A PEACENIK, AREN'T YOU?
RESOLUTION
OCCASIONALLY... ER – HOW WAS YOUR GOOSEBERRY CROP THIS YEAR?
"....ON AND ON AT ME....
"...TILL, IN THE END I CRACKED!"
WELL.... BY THE WAY, DID YOU HOLIDAY ABROAD THIS YEAR?
OKAY, OKAY, I CONFESS! – AND I'D LIKE SEVERAL OTHER CASES OF OPPOSITION TO REAGAN, SOLIDARITY WITH NICARAGUA AND SUPPORT FOR TONY BENN TO BE TAKEN INTO CONSIDERATION!
OH, I SEE.. SO YOU WANT THE RUSSIANS TO INVADE US DO YOU?
LATER...
I'M SORRY MUM – I DID TRY!
NOT TO WORRY, SON – YOUR SISTER'S DIVORCING THE MORON ANYWAY!
SURPRISE ENDING.

RIGHT, LADIES.... THIS WEEK'S TALK, "GOD IS A WOMAN," WILL BE GIVEN BY OUR OWN MRS. PICKERING, WHO ALSO, NOT UNREASONABLY, REFUSED TO LAY ON TONIGHT'S REFRESHMENTS.
BEAM
TEA
W.I. AGENDA
CLAP CLAP

-LOOK- YOU'RE ONLY BEING LIKE THIS 'COS YOUR MOTHER'S HERE! ...I'VE MADE THE PUNCH.. -CAN I PLEASE GO AND FINISH TYPING UP THE AGM MINUTES?
NEVER MIND THE LABOUR PARTY - CONCENTRATE ON THIS PARTY!.... GO AND CIRCULATE.
WHY ARE WE WAITING..
WHAT TIME DOES THE KNEES-UP START?
£29.95
£4.95

WE WERE JUST INCOMPATIBLE REALLY, ...HE INSISTED ON A TOG RATING OF 14 FOR THE DUVET, EVEN IN SUMMER!
?
MEN ARE SUCH SWINE!

GREAT RAILWAY JOURNEYS OF THE WORLD
Nº7: STAINES TO SWINDON
GOD-I'M SO BORED I'VE READ THE ENTIRE CONTENTS OF MY WALLET THREE TIMES ALREADY.
TOILET BUNGED UP
....YES, WHAT WITH MY EXECUTIVE TRAVEL ALLOWANCE AND THESE PERSIL TICKETS, I'M LAUGHING, KEN.
KEN
BEEP-BEEP

* YOUNG UTTERLY PREPARED AND CONCERNED ADULTS

HOME MOVIES

-READY FOR THE FILM EVERYONE?.. IT'S A SEVEN-CHAPTER SPECULATION ABOUT MEMORIES ON THE EDGE OF LANGUAGE. IT'S FULL OF SPLICES, SO IT MIGHT GET STUCK IN THE PROJECTOR, BUT ANYWAY, HOPE YOU LIKE IT. LIGHTS PLEASE SOMEONE, IF YOU'D BE SO KIND........
CANNES NEXT YEAR, EH DEREK?
IS THIS THE ONE WITH YOUR MOTHER AND ME IN?
PSST.... GLENDA, -TIME TO MAKE AN EXCUSE AND LEAVE.

HAS IT REALLY COME TO THIS? JILL'S SITTING IN THE KITCHEN LISTENING TO DESERT ISLAND DISCS...THE KIDS ARE WATCHING GAME FOR A LAUGH IN THE SO-CALLED LIVING ROOM.....I COULD ALWAYS FEED THE GOLDFISH I SUPPOSE...

Special Pedal Steel Supplement
ADVENTURES IN THE 4TH DIMENSION
NO QUIBBLE GUARANTEE
"I WAS WORKING ON MY Ph.D. IN THE DEN WHEN MY DAUGHTER JANE AND HER INTENDED CALLED IN ON THEIR WAY OUT..."
Modern Wall Cupboard
YOU'RE NOT GOING OUT LOOKING LIKE THAT, SURELY?
GOD... DID I SAY THAT?
BOY NEXT DOOR
GIS A BREAK, DAD - WE'RE LINGUISTS OF DESIGN! WEREN'T YOU EVER YOUNG YOURSELF?
TRASH CAN
-SCREEN GOES ALL WOBBLY...

"I WAS A BORN ROMANTIC – A REGULAR FREE GIFTS DEPARTMENT!"
WOULD YOU LIKE THIS 3-SPEED SPORTS BIKE FOR YOUR BIRTHDAY?
OH DEAR, I DON'T WANT TO GET SERIOUS.
FADING MEMORIES
" AND TEENAGE PARTIES WERE ALWAYS AN ORDEAL".
...YES, I CAN CERTAINLY HOLD MY DRINK THESE DAYS... DO YOU FANCY A SNOG?
NO THANKS
GOD! I WISH THE WOMENS' MOVEMENT WOULD HURRY UP AND START!
RED LIGHT BULB
BOGI
I'M A ROADRUNNER HONEY...
LET'S FACE IT, I CAN'T EVEN PUT MY ARM ROUND YOU WITHOUT DEVELOPING CRAMP!

"LUCKILY I FOUND MYSELF A HOBBY...
HI DADDY-O... HEY MAN, LIKE IS IT COOL IF I BUNK OFF EARLY?... IN TEN MINUTES I GOTTA SKIFFLE PRACTICE BEHIND THE BIKE SHEDS.
HMM... THINK I'LL WRITE A BOOK ON POPULAR CULTURE..
E=mc²
SURE, KID, ...AS LONG AS YOU DONT CALL THAT STUFF MUSIC!
"LATER CAME MY PROTEST PERIOD... I WAS THE HIT OF MANY A STUDENT PARTY."
♫ FROM THE ELEVATORS OF EUPHORIA BEHIND THE CURTAINS OF OUR MINDS.. ♪
I'LL BOOK HIM FOR THE FRESHER'S BALL.
-NO, I'M A POST-HEGELIAN ACTUALLY.
DONOVAN HAT→
UNION BAR
CHANGCHANGACHANGACHA...

"FOR A TIME, OUR SOFT ROCK BAND WAS QUITE BIG ON THE ARTS LAB CIRCUIT.."
HOW'S THE JOHN CAGE ONE GO?
FORGET THE WORDS, FORGET THE MUSIC— JUST PLAY... IT'S THE PROCESS THAT MATTERS
READ ALL ABOUT IT! IMAGINATION AS ENERGY! SCIENTOLOGY LATEST!
NO PASSOUTS
SUNSHINE OF YOUR LOVE
VOX
WOW! MY PIANO JUST TURNED INTO THE MILKY WAY!
"THEN I WENT OFF THE RAILS A BIT..."
SHALL I DO THE TON THROUGH THE ODEON SCREEN FOR LAUGHS?
BE CAREFUL— THEY'RE SHOWING A BERGMAN RETROSPECTIVE.

"SO I TOOK TIME OFF-TO DISCOVER WHO I REALLY WAS!"
1ST FLOOR MILLION DOLLAR GURU LTD. MEDITATION. ANALYSIS SITAR LESSONS
I DON'T CARE IF HE DOES HAVE A NUMBERED BANK ACCOUNT IN SWITZ-ERLAND.... HE'S CERTAINLY DOING MY HEAD A LOT OF GOOD!

"BUT MY COMEBACK WAS BLIGHTED... I LACKED STREET CREDIBILITY AND MY CAREER WENT INTO DECLINE..."
I CAN'T HEAR YA! I SAID- DO YA FEEL AAAAAAAAAALLL RIGHT?
CAN'T YOU PLAY ANYTHING FAST?
MAIN STAGE
YOUR LYRICS LACK SOCIO-POLITICAL AWARENESS MISTER, AND YOUR RIFFS ARE INTERMINABLE!
HMM... WE COULD DO 'STAIRWAY TO HEAVEN' AGAIN.... OR MAYBE WE SHOULD AIM FOR A MORE M.O.R. APPEAL.

"...PLUS, WE GOT PANNED BY THE CRITICS..."
IS ELEGANCE OUT OF FASHION? ARE STYLE AND STYLUS DIVORCED? AS BARTHES SAYS...
NME
SAY BOSS, CAN YOU LET ME HAVE MY REVIEW COPY OF THE 2 RONNIES LIVE AT THE BUDOKAN BACK?
"NOW WE JUST DO THE OCCASIONAL SOCIAL CLUB GIG, FOR FUN.."
I THINK WE'LL START THE SECOND SET WITH 'TIE A YELLOW RIBBON', FOLLOWED BY THE BEATLES MEDLEY.
CROWN TOPPER
I HEAR 'ARENA' WILL BE FILMING HERE NEXT WEEK.
LUCKY DRAW 10.15
'ERE MATE, DO YER DO 'VIVA ESPÃNA'?
I THOUGHT THE BAND WERE ADMIRABLY URGENT FOR A CLAPPED-OUT COMBO.
The Ted

FLASH FORWARD.
GOSH, MR. BRENT, - IM SORRY - I DIDN'T MEAN TO UPSET YOU!
NO OFFENCE, SON... YOU SHOULD HEAR WHAT MY OTHER SIBLINGS SAY ABOUT ME! (SEE BELOW, FANS.)
ROXY
IF MY DAD TELLS ME ONE MORE TIME THAT WE ARE THE CHILDREN OF MARX AND COCA-COLA I'LL HIT HIM OVER THE HEAD WITH ONE OF HIS NEIL YOUNG RECORDS.
POETRY OF PROTEST
COFFEE BAR
I KNOW - PARENTS CAN BE SO GROSS.
Teenage Survival Kit

EPILOGUE

Y'KNOW, FRIENDS, - EACH OF US HAS A CROSS TO BEAR.... A CHAP CAME UP TO ME THE OTHER DAY, AS I WAS EMPTYING THE ASH-TRAYS IN THE GARDEN OF REMEMBRANCE, AND SAID, "VICAR, I JUST DON'T FEEL ANY SENSE OF FULFILLMENT IN MY LIFE". SO I SAID TO HIM, MAN TO MAN SO TO SPEAK, "LOOK, MY SON, EACH OF US HAS A CROSS TO BEAR, SO CLEAR OFF."
SNIP SNIP
IN LOVING MEMORY